THIS BOOK IS CLOSED!

by Jeff Whitcher

www.whatifballoons.com

To Matthew

Hello there.

I am very sorry, but this book is closed today.

Please come back tomorrow.

I'm not kidding.

Didn't you read the cover?

This book is **closed**.

There is nothing here to read.

Seriously.

Nothing but blank pages.

Okay, that's enough.

Time to close the book and put it away.

Right **now**.

Let me explain something.

This book is **closed** to the public.

That means only **certain** people are not allowed inside and **you** are not one of them.

Please close the book and put it **back** on your bookshelf.

What do you not understand about what I just told you?

The person who was going to write this book called in sick today.

There is absolutely **nothing** here to read.

The only thing you will find on these pages are germs.

PLEASE close the book and go **wash your hands**.

Thank you.

This isn't funny.

The author of this book is
sick.

He has the flu and is probably
throwing up.

Now *you* are getting his
germs and maybe soon you
will start feeling **sick** too.

You might even get diarrhea.

Gross.

Did you even wash your
hands?

The person who is supposed to be writing this book put me in charge of making sure **no one** trespasses here while he is gone. If he finds out you were going through his book while he was away I am going to be in **big** trouble.

You don't even care, do you?

That is just mean.

I'm sorry if you bought this book thinking there was an interesting story inside, but as you can see there is nothing here.

Now please do as I ask and shut the book immediately.

You're still reading?

You know what?

I don't even care anymore.

Go ahead.

See for yourself.

Turn the next page.

That's right.

Keep turning pages.

It doesn't bother me at all.

Knock yourself out.

Are you feeling sick yet?

Oh, for crying out loud.

WHAT

DO

YOU

WANT

?

Hey, did you hear that?

I think someone is knocking
at your door.

You had better put down the
book and go answer it.

Hurry!

What do I have to do to get you to leave this book alone?

Do me a favor.

Find a grown up and ask
them to come here.

I'll wait while you find a
grown up.

I'm waiting.

Did you find one?

Are you a grown up?

Please do me a favor and take this book away from the child who is reading it. I have been *trying* to tell them that **the book is closed today** but they do not believe me.

Thank you.

Please put the book down now.

Excuse me.

I am trying to be *extremely* **polite** and **nice** about this but I'm beginning to lose my patience.

<u>THIS BOOK IS CLOSED!</u>

I bet you didn't even get a grown up like I asked you to.

It's still **you** reading this book, isn't it?

This is **<u>not</u>** funny.

You are going to get both of us in trouble.

Uh oh.

Did you hear that?

I think someone is coming.

HIDE!

Are you hiding?

I think the coast is clear, but that was *very* close!

If you leave now I promise I won't tell anyone you were here.

Whoops.

You are going the wrong way.

Head that way.

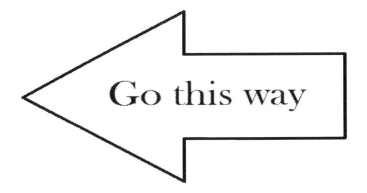

Go this way

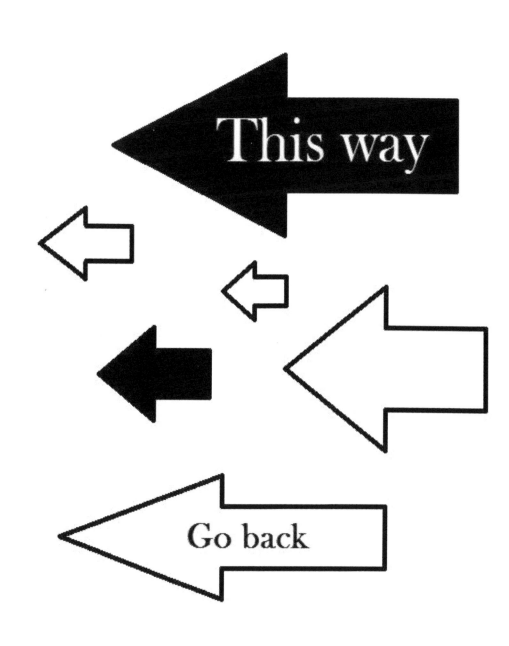

Nope.

You are going in the wrong direction.

Go backwards, not forwards.

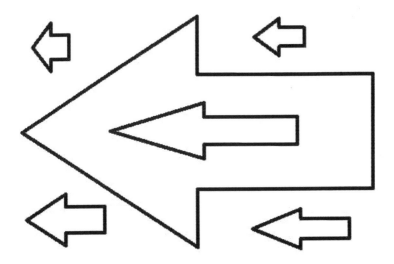

Fine.

If you will **not** put the book down I am going to have to fill the rest of the pages with *VERY* **silly** words that don't make *any* sense and that are **<u>impossible</u>** to read.

FLUNCHBOOGER

SPLODBaTT

CRUDSPANKER

Grustigrumpf

KACKMEISTER

Pipsheebawooboo

PBLUMPBONG

Shoemungus

ZEETBOB

Bonkatonkychunkstinker

Wickydonga deedlediddy joobajibbaki ckykack

Are you **still** here?

You are, aren't you?

I can see you.

I guess there is no point in asking you to stop reading now.

No matter what I say you are going to hang around here bothering me.

Okay, here's an idea.

Let's play a game.

On the count of **three**, I want you to *drop* the book and **run as far away as you can** and I will try and find you.

Ready?

1

2

(Put the book down and hide!)

I think you did not run very far because I can **see** that you are **still** reading this book.

Okay, **I give up.**

We are both in *very* big trouble now because at any minute the person who was supposed to write this book is going to come back and when he sees all your dirty, grimy fingerprints on these pages he is going to know that someone besides me has been here and he will be **super** angry.

You don't look the least bit afraid.

In fact, are you laughing at me?

You are almost to the last page.

If you could go back and wipe all your germy, dirty fingerprints off the pages that would make me very happy.

Wait a minute. You aren't thinking of reading this *again* are you?

No No No No No No **NO!**

Don't even **THINK** about going back to the front of the book and opening it again.

You have already caused me enough grief for one day.

You are *such* a stinker.

The end.

(GO AWAY!!!!)

The person who was supposed to write this book is Jeff Whitcher. He has written many other delightful books for children that you ought to read instead of this one.

53940319R00068

Made in the USA
San Bernardino, CA
02 October 2017